Secret of the Healing Treasures

Secret of the Healing Treasures

Adapted from the Tibetan Epic Tale of Gesar

by Dharma Publishing staff

Illustrated by Julia Witwer

DHARMA PUBLISHING

King Gesar Series

Hero of the Land of Snow
Secret of the Healing Treasures

Library of Congress Cataloging-in-Publication Data

Secret of the healing treasures / adapted from the Tibetan epic tale
  of Gesar by Dharma Publishing staff ; illustrated by Julia Witwer.
      p.   cm. — (King Gesar series)
  Sequel to: Hero of the land of snow
  Summary: In his quest to free an enslaved kingdom from powerful magicians
and release its wondrous healing herbs, young King Gesar must conquer a nine-
headed snake and save a wise princess.
  ISBN 0-89800-217-6 (cloth). — ISBN 0-89800-216-8 (pbk.)
  1. Gesar (Legendary character)—Juvenile literature.
  2. Mythology. Tibetan—Juvenile literature.   3. Gesar (Legendary
character) 4. Mythology. Tibetan.   I. Witwer, Julia, ill.
  II. Dharma Publishing.   III. Gesar   English.   IV. Series.
  BL1950.T5S43   1996
  398.2′0951′502—dc21   96-48214 CIP AC

Printed in the USA by Dharma Press

Dedicated to the compassionate heart

within each of us

Young Gesar, King of Ling, a land high in the snowy mountains of Tibet, had been meditating alone in a cave for several months on how best to serve his kingdom and his people.

Early one spring morning the Goddess Manene, his guardian spirit, suddenly appeared in a brilliant burst of light.

"Arise, Gesar!" Manene cried. "You have done well. You have won your birthright as king and are ready to serve your people. Now the time has come to free a land far to the south. Your mission will help all people who are ill and suffering and prepare you to defeat the Demon of the North."

Manene continued, "King Lungjapa and his wicked magicians have been hoarding all the healing herbs that grow on the hills to the south and are using the magic of the plants to increase their own evil power. Once all the people could use these wonderful leaves and roots, but now the sick and old cannot afford them, and many people are dying. You must free these medicines and release the people, who have been turned into slaves by their evil king."

Gesar emerged from his cave and stood straight and tall. "I am ready to begin!" he cried.

"Your task is not simple, Gesar," said Manene. "A nine-headed tortoise and a nine-headed snake guard the evil magicians' powers. First you must slay these two monsters and carry their magical jewels away. Then you must enter the solid bronze fortress of King Lungjapa and capture the essence of the healing medicines. And finally, you must rescue King Lungjapa's daughter, the princess Pema Chotso. She will help you accomplish your mission."

The dazzling light faded and Manene disappeared.

Gesar reflected for a few moments on the task before him. Then he left his winter cave and returned to his people, a clear purpose and firm resolve now in his heart.

When the people of Ling saw their beloved king approaching on his marvelous horse Kyanshay, they rushed out to greet him.

"Gesar! Gesar!" they shouted. "Welcome back to Ling!" And men, women, and children gathered from all sides to join in welcoming their king.

Gesar dismounted from Kyanshay and greeted his people, calling each one by name. Then he gently told them about the task Manene had given him. The time had come for him to free the people of the south and bring their healing herbs back to Ling.

"But Gesar, you've been gone all winter long! How can you leave us again so soon?" the people cried.

Brougmo, Gesar's beautiful young queen, pleaded, "Dear Gesar, my father is old and weak, and we are counting on you to protect us. Please stay here as our king!"

And all the people of Ling begged Gesar to remain.

Then, from the middle of the crowd, an old man spoke up in a clear, ringing voice: "Gesar, you must do as you are asked. Your destiny calls you—the same destiny that made you our king. Go to the south, free the people, and bring the gift of their medicines back to Ling. Your power protects us against enemies, but we have no protection against disease. In the end, we will all benefit from your open heart and your compassionate actions."

The old man's wise words calmed the crowd, and the people began to understand why Gesar must leave them again so soon.

"Brougmo, my queen, will you look after our kingdom until I return?" asked Gesar. Brougmo accepted, and Gesar blessed the people of Ling and then set off on his journey.

Gesar mounted his wondrous horse Kyanshay and soared high into the sky. Kyanshay, the 'All-Knowing One', was no ordinary stallion. His glossy coat was ruby red, and his blue-black mane and tail flowed behind him like silk banners when he ran. He could fly like the wind and was blessed with human speech and a compassionate heart. "My lord, I am ready to help you in any way I can," said Kyanshay.

So Gesar transformed Kyanshay into a majestic eagle, and together they flew far beyond the peaks of Ling to the lands of the south. There Gesar found a cave called the Cave of Radiant Sunlight where he stayed for a while, preparing to conquer the two nine-headed beasts. The guardians of the evil magicians came in the dark of night and tried to overpower him, but through his magical powers and his clear intent, Gesar conquered them and transformed them into his helpers.

Not far from the cave lived the nine-headed tortoise. Its ancient shell was so enormous it covered a whole valley and so thick it darkened the sky. Its huge toenails dug deep into the earth, creating dangerous pits and cracks that swallowed up any creature that came near. Its nine heads reached up to the treetops, moving constantly, alert to any danger. In an instant, the nine heads could pull back and disappear under the huge protective shell.

Gesar moved silently under the trees until he drew close to the giant beast. Suddenly he gave a mighty cry so powerful that it blew like a hurricane across the tortoise's nine heads. In that instant, the tortoise froze in amazement, and Gesar threw his iron dagger.

The dagger flew like a lightning bolt straight into the tortoise's heart, reducing the huge creature to a heap of dust.

In the heap Gesar found a brilliant crystal. Remembering Manene's advice, he kept it for future use.

Once more Gesar transformed Kyanshay into a giant eagle and flew off to the misty forest in the mountain valley where the snake demon lived.

As Gesar and Kyanshay descended from the clouds into the forest, they entered mist and fog so thick that they could barely see the huge trees that shadowed the earth. In a hollow in a giant tree trunk, Gesar found shelter for the night.

The nine-headed serpent-demon, sensing that a stranger had come into his realm, grew restless and began to roar. Its roaring was louder than an erupting volcano. Throughout the night, the roaring continued without stopping. The earth trembled and the trees moved back and forth.

In the dim light of morning, the serpent crept outside its lair, searching for the stranger, its nine heads coiled and weaving from side to side. Hissing and roaring, it bared its dangerous fangs and darted its poisonous tongues like lightning. The snake sought out any sign of danger, ready to strike at the slightest movement, its eyes glistening in the gloomy darkness.

Gesar took up his golden bow and sheaf of arrows and followed the sound of roaring to the serpent's den. As he drew near, his golden armor shimmering in the misty shadows, the great beast roared even louder.

Gesar focused so fully on his purpose that there was no room for error. Quickly, before the snake could move to strike, Gesar aimed an arrow directly at its heart. The arrow sped true to its course, and in an instant, the serpent collapsed and disappeared.

Only its fangs, eyes, and heart remained, now revealed as marvelous jewels. Gesar collected them all, protecting their magical powers until the time was right to use them.

Outside King Lungjapa's bronze fortress, the gentle people worked in the fields, gathering the medicine plants under the angry watch of their cruel rulers. Each worker had to fill a daily quota or risk being punished. But a worker who was ill was not allowed to use any of the healing herbs. Even a mother was not allowed to give a drink of herbs to her child.

Now at the very moment that Gesar conquered the nine-headed snake, three bad omens suddenly appeared inside the fortress.

"What can these strange omens mean? We must find out," murmured one of the magicians.

"We've never seen such things before!" exclaimed another. But even the best magicians could not interpret the signs.

"This must be a message from the gods of our ancestors," said King Lungjapa. "The gods speak more clearly in dreams, so tonight before we go to sleep we will ask our gods about these strange signs. Tomorrow we can report on what we discover in our dreams." Everyone agreed and went off to bed.

While they slept, Gesar took the form of a young heavenly spirit and appeared before Lungjapa in a dream.

"O mighty ruler," he said, "do not be frightened by what you think are evil signs. These omens are promises of even greater prosperity. They foretell riches and fame for you and your magicians. Tomorrow a holy messenger will appear before your people to reveal your future."

As the dream faded, the greedy Lungjapa awakened, summoned his followers, and proclaimed, "My people, a heavenly visitor has appeared to me in a dream. We do not need to worry. Good things are in store for us.

"Go quickly now and prepare fine food and drink! Spare no expense, for tomorrow a messenger from our gods will come to tell us the true meaning of these signs. We must make sure that our special visitor receives a splendid welcome."

The next morning Gesar changed Kyanshay into a great white elephant and magically transformed himself into the chief messenger and oracle of the gods, cloaked in the finest silk.

King Lungjapa told his guards to open the gates of the fortress and keep watch for the arrival of the celestial visitor. Inside, a huge crowd had already gathered, waiting expectantly.

While guards scanned the road leading to the fortress, a huge white elephant suddenly appeared in the sky. As soon as the guards saw the elephant, the magicians began to play their musical instruments, and King Lungjapa and his people formed a long procession to greet the messenger.

But the elephant did not stop to receive their greeting. Without even a pause, Gesar flew right over the fortress walls and landed in the middle of the courtyard. Everyone was stunned. The surprised musicians put down their instruments and crowded around Gesar.

Gesar broke the hushed silence. "Friends, I have been summoned by the great powers to appear before you. Normally, I give advice only to the gods, who rely on me to foretell the future. What I foretell always comes to pass. Today you have the extraordinary good fortune to learn your own future. Let us proceed to the great hall where I will cast the stones that tell what is to come."

King Lungjapa nodded his head in approval and motioned his followers to present the special gifts. Fruits and sweets, precious jewels, scented flowers, and rich brocades were offered to Gesar as he entered the hall.

The old magician Nopa, standing to one side, eyed Gesar suspiciously. Around Gesar he seemed to see a mist, and beneath the mist another form, clad in shining armor.

"This messenger is not what he seems," thought Nopa, and he challenged Gesar's understanding of magic and philosophy, asking him question after question.

But Gesar answered each challenge without hesitation, prompted by the guardians he had conquered during his stay in the Cave of Radiant Sunlight. When Gesar explained complicated theories that Nopa himself had not mastered, everyone applauded and cheered. Even Nopa could not help but be impressed by the oracle's intelligence and understanding.

Now a special cloth painted with a symbolic map of the region was spread on the floor of the great hall. Gesar shook the golden vase that held the stones that foretold the future. Out tumbled a white stone, which landed in the center where the fortress was pictured. Gesar interpreted, "Your fortress will always be protected."

Next, two speckled stones fell in another spot, and Gesar proclaimed, "The field workers will become strong."

A tiny white stone richocheted off the cloth. Gesar thundered, "Your sage Nopa has doubted me. He must apologize at once!"

Then six small stones scattered in all four directions, and Gesar was silent. After a while he said in a grave voice, "You are threatened by a great danger from Tibet. A powerful warrior is on his way to destroy your healing plants."

He paused and then said, "But you can avoid this danger by using these plants as protection.

"Listen carefully: Take all the dried herbs out of your store-houses and pile them up high around the outside of the fortress. Then wait for my return."

With a large, sweeping gesture, Gesar threw the stones one last time. He looked at the stone that fell on the cloth and warned, "Do not become confused. Do not be misled by emotion or fear."

Gesar took Lungjapa aside and advised, "Your daughter will have bad dreams and will become upset. She will doubt these predictions. Do not listen to her. Heed my words well, for your lives are at stake."

Then Gesar disappeared into the clouds on his flying elephant, leaving only a white rainbow trailing off into space.

Amazed and shaken by what Gesar had said, King Lungjapa and his people followed the oracle's instructions to the letter. They took all the dried medicines out of their storerooms and piled them up around the rim of the fortress until they reached the height of the great outer wall.

That night the Princess Pema Chotso tossed and turned in her bed. In the morning she rushed to her father's chambers, her eyes wide and her face pale.

Trembling, Pema said, "Father, I have had terrible dreams of disaster to our kingdom. I dreamed that the sun grew hotter and hotter, and the snow melted on the mountains. I saw the walls of the fortress covered with flames as hot as the sun. I heard the winds howl and saw the flames rise up to the sky!"

King Lungjapa thought to himself, "What the oracle predicted is already coming true!"

"Father, I saw our visitor in my dream! He was riding a chest-nut horse and wearing a suit of armor. He is not to be trusted—he is an impostor!"

"There, there, child," said King Lungjapa. "You're just imagining these terrible things. They are not real. You musn't let yourself be carried away by childish fears."

"But father, our kingdom is in danger. You must listen to me!"

"The oracle warned us that you would have bad dreams. But these dreams are not to be taken seriously," said Lungjapa. "Pema Chotso, go to your room and calm down. Leave me at once and do not speak of this again!"

Alone in her room, Pema sobbed, "Alas, my father cannot hear me. I'm trying to save him and our people, but his ears are deaf and his eyes are blind."

Meanwhile, Gesar had retreated to the nearby Cave of Radiant Sunlight where he transformed himself into a beautiful goddess and Kyanshay into a crystal scepter. Mounting the crystal scepter, he appeared in an instant in Pema Chotso's room.

Pema Chotso had fallen asleep and was dreaming that she was in the presence of a divine being. She awoke with a start and was amazed to find the room bathed in rainbow light. A beautiful god-dess hovered in mid-air, while heavenly music played softly.

"Sweet sister, do not be afraid," said Gesar. "Our common celestial father is watching over you. He has brought you a gift, a crystal scepter, and the message that your stay in this land is for a good purpose. You must guard this crystal scepter carefully, for it will help you escape when the time is right."

Pema was reassured by the lovely goddess and offered her food and drink and a rare turquoise the color of the sky of India.

Gesar said, "Princess Pema, I would like to ask you one favor. Your people possess a very special herb that grants the power to live forever. It is the essence of all the healing plants. May I see it before I go?"

Now Pema had sworn to her father that she would never show this treasured herb to anyone. But she was so grateful to the goddess and so convinced of her sincerity that she went to get the small golden box hidden in her inner chamber. Its special lock and key were made of a beautiful blue gem.

As Pema turned the key in the lock and lifted the lid, rays of light shot forth from the miraculous leaves within. The light was so brilliant that for an instant she was bedazzled. In that moment, Gesar used his magical powers to remove the herb from the box and put an imitation in its place. He hid the real treasure in his garments.

Gesar smiled and thanked Pema for her kindness in showing him the special herb. Pema carefully closed the box, having noticed nothing unusual, and bade farewell to the goddess, who suddenly disappeared.

Gesar returned to the Cave of Radiant Sunlight and meditated on the final steps needed to accomplish his mission.

After five days and nights, the sun and moon and stars, the mountains and the woods gave him signs that the moment had come to complete the destruction of the evil magicians' power and act for the good of all.

He traveled to the fortress and blew three times upon a trumpet. Then five magical forms, each one an exact resemblance of him, sprang forth from his side.

Four of these magical forms streamed like rays of light to the fortress, each to one of the four directions. Flames leaped from their bodies, and tongues of fire from their feet crept along the ground, as though the earth itself were spitting fire.

Suddenly the wind rose and the mounds of medicine plants burst into flames. Within seconds the entire tower was burning out of control. Howling winds whipped the blaze into a raging fire-storm. Fireballs exploded high in the sky and billows of thick smoke darkened the horizon all the way to India and China. People there asked their magicians the meaning of the murky darkness and prayed for protection against a disaster.

Meanwhile, Gesar's fifth magical form flew to Princess Pema's chambers in the innermost recesses of the fortress. Pema was not frightened when the magical form appeared and knew what to do without being told. She stepped lightly onto the crystal scepter, which was actually Gesar's flying horse, Kyanshay, and rode away from the fortress to Gesar's cave.

As she stood before Gesar she saw his five magical forms reunite into a rainbow and flow back into his body. Pema gazed at this magical being, her eyes shining with wonder and awe.

Gesar said, "Princess Pema, do not be afraid. Now I can tell you who I really am.

"I am Gesar, King of Ling. I came here to free you and your people from the spell of the evil magicians. Once the magical healing plants grew freely on the land and were used by all the people. But the magicians and your father became greedy. They hoarded the plants and kept secret the knowledge of how to use them. They used the magic of the herbs to increase their own evil power and turned the people into slaves.

"Now the power of this greed has been broken. The people are freed, and the healing plants can once more be used by all."

As Pema Chotso looked at Gesar, she saw the shining armor of a kingly warrior. His compassionate smile warmed her heart and filled her with hope.

The wise princess saw that the selfish cruelty of her father and his magicians had caused the people much suffering, and she was glad that the magical healing herbs could now by used by anyone who needed them.

Gesar and the princess returned to the bronze fortress, which had miraculously survived the great fire. Gesar shot an arrow at the walls, and they flew apart, revealing hidden books of learning that had been buried deep in the ground.

Gesar kept some of the books and gave some to Pema Chotso for safekeeping. Then Gesar and Pema flew back to the Cave of Radiant Sunlight.

"Soon I will reveal the teachings found at the fortress to a good king who lives nearby," said Gesar. "From there, they will be distributed widely.

"Deep in this cave there is a casket of gold that holds books of magical knowledge. Pema Chotso, now is the time for you to become the guardian of these teachings. First you must spend a month here being my student. Then you must stay on retreat in this cave for three years, practicing these teachings until you completely master them."

Pema's heart filled with joy. She said softly, "Gesar, there is nothing I want more than this. I thank you with all my heart for the chance to study and practice these wonderful teachings. I will practice day and night until I master them."

For the next month, Gesar and Pema Chotso sat in the cave, teacher and student, absorbing the depth of the teachings in the precious books that had been buried in the cave.

Then Gesar said, "It is time for me to finish my task and return to the kingdom of Ling. Farewell, Pema Chotso! Do not forget what I have taught you. Study and practice faithfully. In three years you will be ready to teach others."

Gesar mounted Kyanshay and rode to a neighboring kingdom ruled by a good king. There he took the form of a learned scholar and transformed Kyanshay into his servant.

The king was amazed at the sudden appearance of such a learned teacher in his kingdom and immediately invited Gesar to his court. He honored Gesar with the finest foods, and offered him silken robes, gold, and precious jewels.

"Great learned one," the king said, "please accept my invitation to stay here in my kingdom and teach at my court."

So Gesar stayed for a while, teaching from the books saved from the fortress. He taught harmony, balance, and an enlightened way of living based on love, compassion, and wisdom.

The king and his people soon learned to live joyfully, with open hearts, loving all beings like their own children. They no longer brought harm to one another, and the powers of evil faded away from their hearts and minds. The good king wished all his subjects well and did everything he could to increase their happiness. The people's hearts grew light and their faces bright and cheerful.

Nature responded to their love and compassion like a flower to the sun. The seasons followed one another harmoniously, and the earth produced all kinds of delicious fruits and vegetables. Pure

blue water filled the lakes and ponds, and the medicine plants, now freely available, covered the hillsides with their sweet-smelling leaves and flowers. Swarms of bees hovered in mid-air, attracted to their blossoms, while the echoing calls of birds filled the air with sweet song.

The king honored Gesar as the best of teachers and bestowed upon him the name Lion of the World. He then offered Gesar eighty-four thousand bales of medicine herbs to take back with him to Ling. The people of the kingdom gladly harvested the herbs, gathered them into bales, and gave the bales to Gesar, grateful for the things he had taught them.

To help Gesar transport the plants back to Ling, the king's ministers transformed themselves into great eagles. Then they picked up the sacks of healing herbs in their talons and flew to Ling overnight, placing the sacks on the roof of Gesar's palace.

Gesar rejoiced, for his task was now complete. He bid farewell to everyone, saying,

"After three years have passed, go to the Cave of Radiant Sunlight at the end of the Valley of the Highest Medicines. There you will find a lady who practices magical healing arts for the benefit of people everywhere.

"She will have matted hair, but a great light will shine all around her. Tell her that the Lion of the World sends his blessing and that it is time for her to teach for the welfare of all.

"You yourself, O King, should take her as your highest teacher and always serve her with respect and devotion."

The king promised to do as Gesar instructed, and he and his entire court accompanied Gesar halfway back to Ling.

That night, Manene appeared to Brougmo, Gesar's wife, in a dream. Brougmo dreamed that she was being entertained by beautiful princesses in a heavenly palace. Suddenly, the princess Manene turned to her and said, "Tomorrow a hero is coming to Ling. Don't forget about him—you don't want to be unprepared!" Then she and the other princesses disappeared like a rainbow into space.

Immediately Brougmo woke up and found the sun rising. She rose and sent word to all the chiefs of Ling that King Gesar was returning home that day.

When Gesar rode into Ling that afternoon, a royal welcome greeted him. All of Ling had turned out to greet their king.

"Gesar, Gesar, you're back! How wonderful to see you, Gesar!" shouted the first onlookers. But as they saw Gesar coming home in the same way he had left—empty-handed and without any companions—the joy of the people was mixed with concern, for they wondered if he had really accomplished anything.

Gesar knew what his people were thinking, and he had already sent his chiefs to the palace roof. He pointed up to the sky just as the men started throwing down the sacks of healing herbs, and everyone laughed in surprise.

"How wonderful, Gesar! You have brought us the gift of these magical herbs, just as you promised," exclaimed the people.

Then Gesar rejoiced with his queen Brougmo and his countrymen, and all gave prayers of thanks for his safe return and for the gift of the healing herbs. The plants served his people well, guarding them against sickness and disease. Gesar protected the essence of the healing plants and the magical jewels he had taken from the nine-headed monsters, for they would give him special powers in his next adventure.

King Gesar Series

For nearly a thousand years Gesar's adventures have been celebrated in Tibetan legend and song. Hundreds of versions of the Gesar epic exist, in written and spoken form. *Hero of the Land of Snow*, the first book in Dharma Publishing's King Gesar Series, retells the story of Gesar's birth and the great horse race he must win to become King of Ling. This second book takes us on a journey to the wild lands and evil kingdoms to the south of Ling.

The origin of the Gesar epic can be traced through historical records to the eleventh century when a king named Gesar ruled the kingdom of Ling in an area of high peaks and deep river valleys near the Amnye Machin mountains.

Gesar's heroic task is to overcome the dark forces, both inner and outer, that bring war and hardship and obscure the path to enlightenment. Each character in the epic, from the evil king, Lungjapa, to the celestial beings who guide Gesar in his quest, symbolizes a psychological and spiritual force. Gesar harnesses and unifies these forces, just as he unifies the kingdom of Ling. Gesar's ultimate victory promises that peace, harmony, and enlightenment will prevail in the world.

Pronunciation guide: The sound of Tibetan words can be difficult to express in English spelling. Even in Tibet, pronunciation varies from region to region, and there can be several ways to sound out the same word. These general guidelines will help you pronounce the names in this story. Gesar: *Ge* rhymes with *say*, *sar* rhymes with *far*. Brougmo: Brou is pronounced *drew*, and mo is pronounced *mow*, so Brougmo really sounds more like *drewk-mow*. Pema Chotso: *pe* is pronounced *pay*, ma is pronounced *ma*; cho and tso rhyme with *no*. Kyanshay: *kyan* sounds like *key on* and *shay* rhymes with *day*.

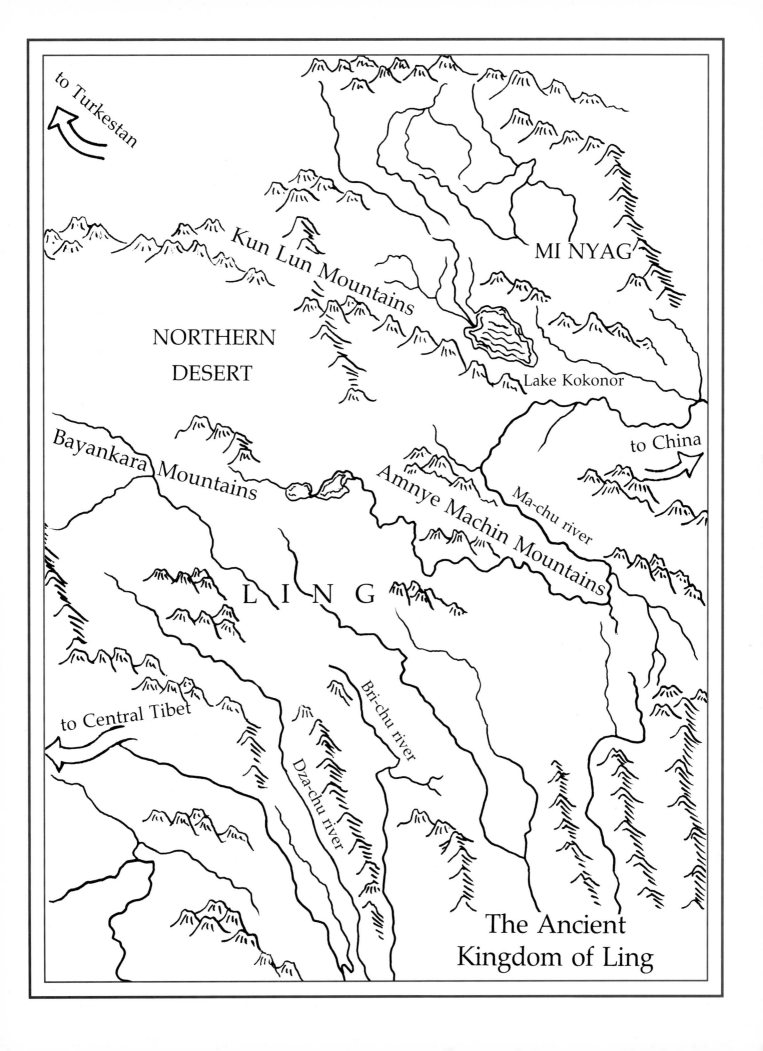